Great-Grandma's Gifts

Written by
Marianne Jones

Illustrated by
Karen Reinikka

ISBN-13: 978-1522758709

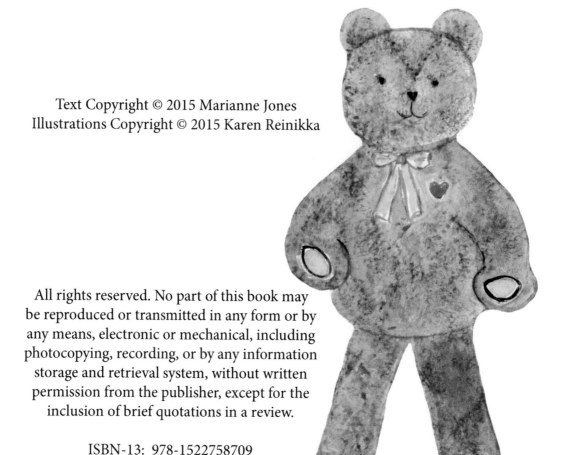

To our mother,
Arlene Hamilton,
and her beloved
great-grandchildren
Andrew, Sonia, Amund and Zoe
with love,

Karen Reinikka
and
Marianne Jones

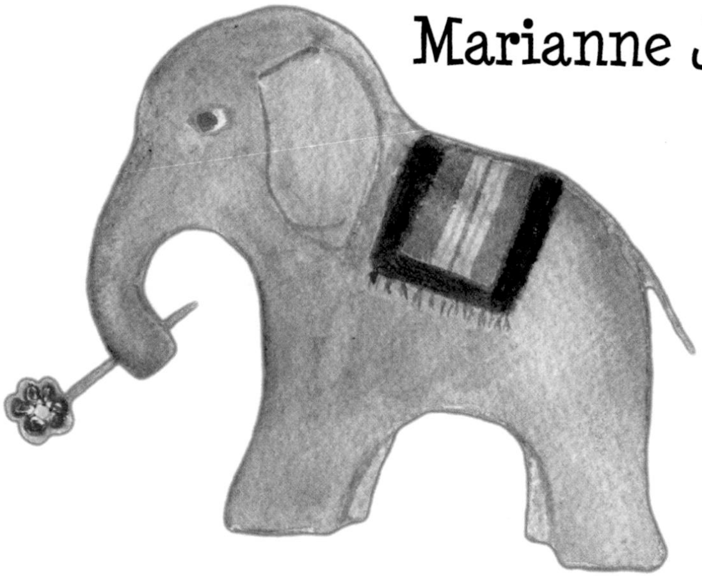

This is a story about my
great-grandma.

She is different from your great-grandma, but there is something very special about all of the great-grandmas in the world.

They have lived a very long time and have many interesting stories.

You see, great-grandmas weren't always grandmas. Mine was once a little girl named Arlene, and she liked to play with dolls.

Her favourite doll was named Maggie.

One day, Arlene's mother bought some red velvet. It was **as red as a valentine** and **as soft as a puppy**.

Arlene asked her mother, "What will you do with that?"

Her mother said, "Wait and see."

Arlene watched her mother cut the velvet and sew the velvet.

Then her mother said, "Come and see."

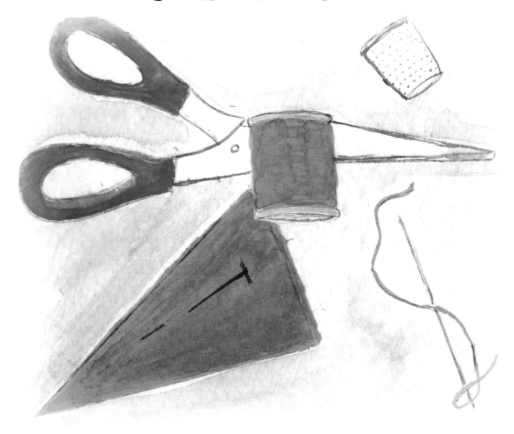

It was a dress,
and it was just
Arlene's size.

It was

as red as a
valentine
and as soft
as a puppy.

Arlene felt pretty in her red dress. Her mother was happy.

Arlene saw pieces of leftover velvet. "May I have them?" she asked.

"Why, what will you do with them?" her mother asked.

"Wait and see," Arlene said.

Arlene cut the velvet, and
pinned it, and sewed it.

Then Arlene said
to her mother,
"Come and see."

It was a dress
just Maggie's
size.

Maggie was
pretty in her
red
dress.

Arlene
was happy.

One day, Arlene's mother bought some silk.

It was

as blue as Arlene's eyes
and as soft as water.

Arlene watched her mother pin, and cut, and sew the silk until she had a top that was **as blue as Arlene's eyes** and as soft as water.

Arlene saw that there were still some pieces left.

"May I have them?" she asked.

"What for?" said her mother.

"It's a surprise," Arlene said.

Arlene pinned the silk, cut it, and sewed it.

When she was finished, she said, "Come and see."

It was a silk pillow for Maggie's bed.
It was **as blue as Arlene's eyes**
and as soft as water.

When Arlene grew up,
she had a baby girl,

and a
baby boy,

and
ANOTHER
baby girl,

and
ANOTHER
baby boy!

Arlene was busy, but she still liked
to sew.

She made coats,

and dresses,

and pants,

and skirts,

and tops.

She had many pieces of cloth left:
red cloth, yellow cloth,
green cloth, and pink cloth.

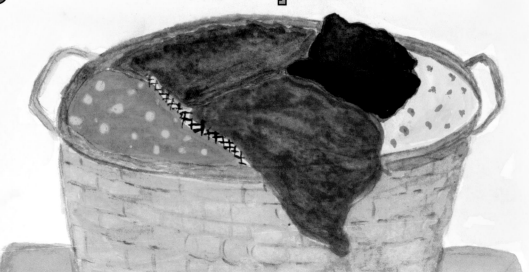

There were **MANY** colours of cloth.

"What will I do with all of these pieces?" Arlene asked.

Then she had an idea.

From a **fuzzy** coat,
she made
a teddy bear.

From a **pink** top, she made a doll.

From a grey dress,
she made an elephant.

Her children were
very happy with
their toys.

Arlene was happy, too.

When
Arlene's
children
grew up,
they had
children of
their own.

Arlene was now a
grandma!

Arlene loved being a grandma.

She had lots of cloth
to make toys.

Her grandchildren loved
Peachy Keen the best.

When the grandchildren grew up, they were too old for toys.

But Arlene still liked to sew.

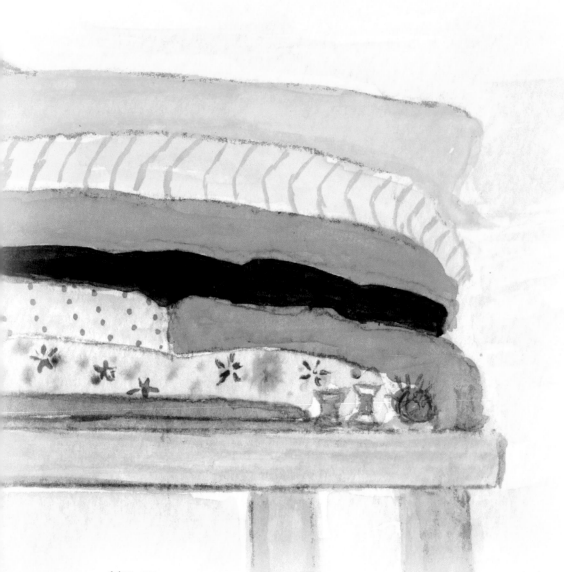

"What will I do now?" she asked.

"I have lots of cloth:
silky black cloth,
sparkly gold cloth,
shiny purple cloth,
cloth with polka dots,
and cloth with stripes."

Then she had an idea.

First she cut old shirts into squares.

Then she cut more pieces of cloth and
sewed them into bigger squares.

When she had many colourful squares, she sewed them together into **BIG** quilts.

It took a long time, but she had fun.

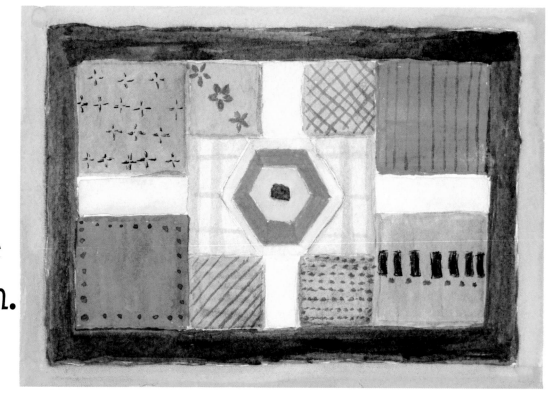

She made quilts for all of her grandchildren.

Everyone said, "What beautiful quilts! Where did you get them?"

They said,

"From our Grandma Arlene."

Arlene's grandchildren said to her,
"What will you do now?"

"I am tired of making things," she said.

"I think I will take a rest."

And that is what she did.

Made in the USA
Coppell, TX
08 May 2022

77559435R00021